Copyright © 2020 Anna Anisimova | Illustrations © 2020 Yulia Sidneva
Translation copyright © 2023 Ruth Ahmedzai Kemp

First published as *Музыка моего дятла* by Samokat, Moscow, 2020

All rights reserved.

First Restless Books hardcover edition August 2023

Hardcover ISBN: 9781632063243 | Library of Congress Control Number: 2022947628

Cover artwork and design by Yulia Sidneva | Typesetting by Tetragon, London

Printed in Italy

1 3 5 7 9 10 8 6 4 2

Restless Books, Inc. | 232 3rd Street, Suite A101 | Brooklyn, NY 11215

restlessbooks.org | publisher@restlessbooks.org

This book is supported in part by an award from the National Endowment for the Arts.

This book is made possible by the New York State Council on the Arts with the support of
Governor Kathy Hochul and the New York State Legislature.

Anna Anisimova

THE INVISIBLE ELEPHANT

Illustrated by Yulia Sidneva

Translated from Russian
by Ruth Ahmedzai Kemp

RESTLESS BOOKS
BROOKLYN, NEW YORK

Contents

Everyone has their unique abilities and possibilities.

When we understand people who are different from us, we're not afraid to talk to them and we don't deprive ourselves of the joy of their friendship.

Isn't that what the world is all about?

1.

We're playing hide-and-seek, and I'm the seeker. I count out loud, up to ten, and then I go and look for Mama.

That's the door. That's the hallway with the bumpy wallpaper. That's the coat rack, all puffed up and full of coats. Mama's not here.

I open the door to the kitchen, and listen carefully. The clock ticks, the fridge rumbles—that's it. I can't hear anyone. But, just in case, I walk over to the kitchen table and feel underneath. Nope—no one there either. There's nowhere else to hide in the kitchen, so I go into the living room.

There's no one behind the living-room door. Or under the sofa, or under the coffee table. I go up to the window, and hear Mama breathing. I pull the curtain across and touch Mama. Found you!

I love hide-and-seek! So what if I know all the hiding places in our house? After all, I'm only allowed to play at home. Still, I really love hide-and-seek! Now it's Mama's turn to be the seeker.

Mama wraps a scarf around her eyes as a blindfold (she likes to play fair), then she starts counting. I walk past the table, the sofa, the door, down the hallway with the bumpy wallpaper.

I go into Mama's bedroom and head over to the big wardrobe. I open the door as quietly as I can. I climb inside and stand as still as I can among Mama's skirts and dresses.

There are so many dresses—it's like a forest! And they all smell so nicely of Mama, that I breathe in her smell . . . I take a deep breath of the Mama forest smell . . .

And I don't even hear her coming, she's so quiet! Mama opens the wardrobe doors, but doesn't say anything. What's wrong?

I reach out to touch her face. Mama's lips are smiling, but her eyebrows are frowning a little. Maybe she's mad because I creased some of her clothes? I quickly smooth down the skirts and dresses, and then give her a huge hug!

Mama strokes my head. No, she's not mad!

2.

Papa and I are off to the museum today. When we go to a museum, we're allowed to touch the stuffed animals, and all the different objects and rocks. Other visitors aren't allowed to touch anything, but we are.

In the first room, Papa puts his hand on my shoulder and talks to the person who works there.

"I'm with my daughter. May we look at the exhibits?" he asks.

"Yes, but be careful," a gloomy voice replies. "We just had a boy crashing around in here. . . . An elephant in a china shop, he was! Touching everything. He knocked over all the spears."

Papa promises the gloomy person that we'll be very careful. But I really want to see this elephant. Where is it? I've never felt one before.

Papa explains that you can only see an alive elephant at the circus or the zoo. And when the man said "an elephant in a china shop," he just meant someone clumsy. Imagine what would happen if one got into the museum! He'd destroy everything.

"Ooh, look at this," says Papa as he leads me along.

He takes my hand and helps me touch something cold, and hard, and very long.

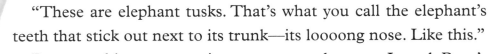

"These are elephant tusks. That's what you call the elephant's teeth that stick out next to its trunk—its loooong nose. Like this."

Papa puts his arm up against my nose to show me. I touch Papa's arm-trunk and try to imagine. . . . How does an elephant walk around with such a long nose? He must trip over it all the time!

"Elephant tusks are very valuable," Papa tells me. "So valuable that people hunt elephants to steal their tusks."

I run my fingers over the tusks and listen carefully to Papa. What incredible teeth! If I had teeth like those, I wouldn't even fit in Mama's wardrobe! Could this elephant really be that enormous?

3.

Papa and I step back into the apartment and right away we smell something yummy in the air. Mama's cooking something! The kitchen is full of steamy air from the oven. Mama says her friend Taika is coming to visit.

"What are you cooking?" I ask.

"Wash your hands and come see," says Mama.

I do what she says. I love having clean fingers. Ready! I stretch out my hands, Mama takes them, and guides me to the warm oven-tray. Ah, bumpy shapes—that feels like cookies. Next to them there's a can—ooh, I know, that might be condensed milk! And next to it on the baking paper there's something greasy and soft . . . hmm, what's that? I lick my finger. Ugh, it's warm butter!

"Anthill cake?" I guess.

"Yes! Well, don't just stand there. Let's get your apron on, then we can get sculpting."

Mama crushes the cookies into a big bowl, and I stir them up with the butter and condensed milk. My fingers are covered in 'anthill' goo! You wouldn't see even an elephant with mucky hands like this!

4.

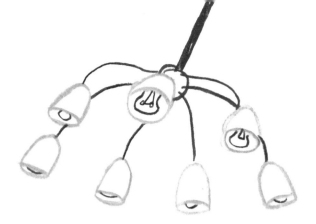

I'm on the balcony waiting for Taika to arrive. I'll know from the smell when she's here! Mama sometimes teases Taika for spraying herself with an entire bottle of perfume. Taika always laughs. Maybe she'll get a job in a puffery . . . no, a perfumery . . . a perfume store! And I would like to work in one with her. I love Taika's perfume! And I love that I can spot her by her scent. She must have a whole closet full of perfume: a new bottle every day. . . .

I'm waiting for the perfume scent. There it is! She's here! I start jumping up and down with excitement. Taika calls up to me from the street.

"Hello! How are you?"

I shout down to her, telling her how I went to the museum and saw an elephant's tusks! Taika shouts back that I'm jumping around like an elephant and should maybe give the balcony a rest—it's wobbling under my feet!

I need to ask Papa to tell Taika that elephants can't even jump. Which is probably for the best. Because if elephants could jump, it wouldn't just be an earthquake, it would be an elephant-quake!

5.

Taika has brought her son with her. He's little. Younger than me, and smaller—you can tell by feeling. But he's noisy! He runs around, stomping. Back and forth. Back and forth. He takes my toys, but he doesn't put them back where he found them. And now everything's scattered all over the place! Like an elephant in a china shop!

I want to show Taika my new music box. I look for it everywhere—it's gone! Taika scolds her son, but he just laughs—he's too little to understand. But Mama quickly finds it, and asks me not to be angry. We'll soon have everything back in its place.

6.

Mama and I tidy up after our guests have gone. It's true—it doesn't take long to get everything back to normal. The way it needs to be. The way I'm used to.

Mama gets out the vacuum cleaner and asks me to clean the carpet. It's not hard for me, so I often do it. I pull out the cord and plug it in. I press the button and vr-oo-oom! The vacuum cleaner starts sucking!

I hold the brush and push it around the carpet. Vr-oo-oom!

All the dust and bits go up the hose, like the vacuum cleaner is sucking up its lunch. . . . Oh yes, the hose is an elephant's trunk! My vacuum cleaner's an elephant, too! Only without the big, flappy ears.

Vr-Oo-oOm!

7.

Mama sings for me at bedtime, before I go to sleep. I'm always a bit scared to be on my own at night. But I'm not scared when I have songs in my head. I love Mama's songs. And I love my elephant, a little bit, anyway. Maybe he's scared of going to sleep on his own, too?

I start singing along with Mama. If my elephant is that huge, and has huge tusks and a huge trunk, that means he must have huge ears, too. So even if he's far away, he'll hear my singing.

Don't be scared, elephant!

8.

It's nearly fall. Mama and I go to the store to buy me some new clothes and shoes. I try on a coat, and feel the big, round buttons. They're nice and smooth. I stick my hands in the pockets—they're nice and deep. I could fill them with chestnuts to play with in secret.

Mama asks me to choose a color. There's a red coat and a green one.

"What kind of red?" I ask.

"Like a tomato," says Mama.

"And what kind of green?"

"Like an apple," Mama says.

Of course, I choose the apple coat! Because apples make a lovely crunch when you bite them, and tomatoes are squashy and squelchy.

"Do elephants eat apples?" I ask Mama.

"They love them! Elephants are herbivores. They eat everything that grows. Grass, apples, carrots. . . ."

I remember the smells of grass, apples, and carrots. Carrots . . . what color are they again? Are they the same color as elephants? I think Papa said they're both gray. A carroty elephant—it sounds beautiful.

Mama gives me some shoes to try on. I'm still thinking about my elephant, and put the right shoe on my left foot, and the left shoe on my right. Oh, what a muddle! My hands just can't work out which shoe is which. I wonder if my elephant also gets muddled up. Does he know which one is his right tusk and which one is his left?

9.

At art class, I sit at my own table, away from the other children. As if I'm an elephant and I need a lot of space.

In fact, Pasha's the one who's like a clumsy elephant. He's always dropping things: pencils, paper, even himself!

Everyone is doing a still life with the teacher, but I'm drawing an elephant. Everyone else is painting with a brush, but I'm using my fingers.

I put both my index fingers side by side on the paper. One stays where it is. The other one does a big circle and comes back to meet the other one again. I do a really BIG circle. Because an elephant is big and fat, because he eats a lot. Now the big tusks. Big ears. Long trunk. . . .

My teacher praises my drawing. Everyone stands around to have a look. That's why there's so much space around me—so everyone can stand by my table to see!

Pasha asks, "I want to do that too! Can I also paint with my fingers?"

But then he drops his paint pot on the floor!

"Pasha!" I hear my teacher's sharp voice.

Then everyone else starts asking. . . .

"Can I do that too?"
"Ooh, I want to paint with my fingers!"
Everyone wants to do what I'm doing. Everyone wants an elephant, too.

10.

At the park, children are running around and playing. Their mamas and grandmas are sitting nearby, chatting, bags rustling. Papa and I are on the grass. We spread out a blanket and sit down. Papa looks up at the sky and tells me what the clouds look like.

"That one's like a hare, or . . . yes, definitely, a hare. There are its long ears."

I can see the clouds perfectly. Papa explained that a cloud is like a huge puff of cotton candy. But without the stick. I'm holding some cotton candy and pulling out two tufts, one on each side. And I know what a hare looks like. Like a rabbit! I saw a rabbit in grandma's village. He was so soft and had long floppy ears.

"Is it like this?" I show Papa my cotton candy hare.

"Exactly!" Papa sounds proud of me.

I'm so happy! You can't touch a cloud hare but you can touch mine, no problem. I lie back on the blanket and lay the hare on my stomach.

"I'm the sky! And my hare is a cloud!" I laugh.

Suddenly the wind appears out of nowhere, and snatches away my laugh. My hare flies away!

"Oh no!" Papa says with a laugh. "The wind's chasing two hares at the same time! It's chased them both away."

I sit up.

"What are the clouds like now?"

Papa looks, and then shouts. "It can't be! It can't be!" He's shouting louder than all the children in the park. I'm so worried, I might fly off after my hare.

"What? What can you see?"

"It's your elephant! Can you imagine? He's up in the sky!"

Papa pulls me back down onto the blanket and laughs. I'm laughing too. I'm so happy! The wind definitely can't chase my elephant out of the sky. My elephant is huge. And if he wants to, he can take a big puff of air with his trunk and blow this silly wind away!

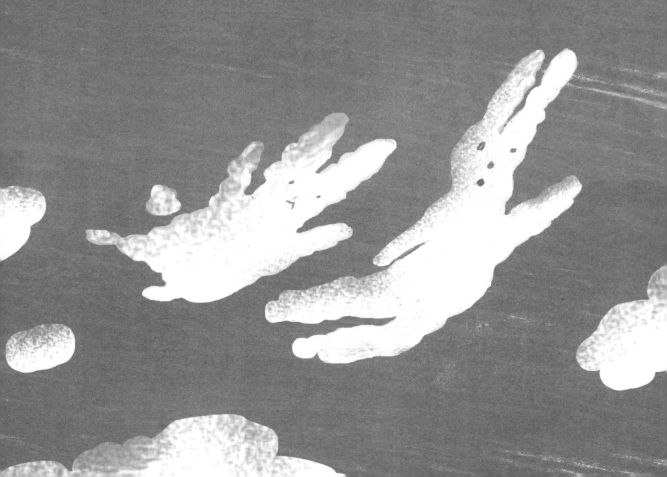

11.

It's the weekend! We're going to the zoo, and I'm going to see a real elephant. I'm so excited I drop Mama and Papa's hands and leap ahead.

"Careful!" says Mama, but she doesn't manage to stop me. "There are boys there playing football!"

I don't listen to her. I make my fist into a trunk. I'm jumping around and trumpeting like an elephant.

"Boo-boo-boo! I'm going to the zoo!"

And the whole world trumpets along with me!

The birds are going twee-twee-twoo!

The cars are going vroo-vroo-vroom!

But then—BOOM!

Ow! My head . . .

I sit down and hold my forehead where the football hit me. I hear it roll away onto the grass.

"Can't you see we're playing here?" I hear a boy shout, then run away.

Mama is beside me. "Does it hurt?" She wraps her arms around me. "It's all right. There, there."

Her fingers are trembling on my shoulders.

I clench my teeth and shake my
head sharply from side to side.
I know that means "no."

Papa is beside me too. "It's OK,
sweetheart," he says. "Did you
know, elephants cry too?"

12.

At the zoo, we go straight to see the elephant. I'm in such a hurry that I don't pay any attention to the pavement, and all the bumps and stones.

But Mama's always on the look-out. "There's a hole on your right. . . . A puddle on your left. . . . Now there's a step down. . . . One more. . . . Careful! One bruise is enough for today!"

But I'm in a hurry. I'm in the lead, and I'm taking Mama and Papa to see the elephant!

Here we are at the enclosure. It's smelly! Mama finds us a space, and lets me pick up some sticks.

"The elephant is on the other side," says Mama. "At the back of the enclosure, there's a ditch with water. And behind that is the playground. The elephant is standing over there. Too far away to reach. But oh, what a biggie! He's taller than you and me put together. He's picking up grass with his trunk and putting it in his mouth. And his ears are like curtains. As big and wide as our curtains! I could easily hide behind them. . . . What else can I tell you?"

Mama hands me a carrot. "Do you want to give him a treat?"

Papa lifts me onto his shoulders. I wave the carrot back and forth, then toss the elephant his carroty treat. I hear a splash.

"The perfect shot!" Papa says, with a laugh. "He'll eat it soon. You'll see!"

But I hear the elephant walk further away, his feet shuffling on the ground.

"He's probably gone for a rest," says Mama. "He's on his feet all day, poor thing."

We stand there a little, and then we also walk away. I turn back to wave goodbye, and I sense the elephant watching me. I can feel him breathing in my direction.

13.

That night, I dream that the elephants are lying on the grass and looking up at the sky. And I'm a cloud drifting across it.

The elephant children ask their Mama: "What does that cloud look like?"

But the elephant Mamas don't reply. Either they don't know, or they're feeling shy.

Then I shout: "They look like you! I'm just like you! I'm an elephant, too! If you jump up, you can hug me with your trunk! Like an arm!"

But the elephants don't jump up. Even in my dream, elephants are too big and heavy to jump!

14.

I'm aN ElePhAnt, tOo!

The doorbell rings. I hear from the footsteps that Papa has gone to answer the door. And then I hear that it's Pasha from my art class. And his Mama. How funny!

"Come in! Come in! You're keeping me from my pie!" says Papa, cheerfully. Then he calls to me. "You've got visitors!"

"I'm coming!" I call back.

Here's the door. The hallway with the bumpy wallpaper. The coat rack, all puffed up and full of coats.

"Hi, Pasha!"

"Hello! I've brought you some play-dough," he replies. And he drops it on the floor. "Oh!"

I laugh. "Pasha, shall I call you Elephant?"

1.

My Grandpa has three legs. Two are quiet and one is noisy, like a woodpecker.

"Shoo, shoo." That's how his quiet legs rustle.

"Tok!" That's the knocking sound the noisy one makes.

Mama and Papa say it's a walking stick. But Grandpa says it's a leg—the fittest leg in the world. I look at it with my hands. It's long and thin, like a normal stick, but ever so smooth. And at the top it has a handle, curved like half a bagel!

"If it's a leg, why does it have a handle? Do legs usually have handles?" I ask my Grandpa.

"It's not a handle, it's a finger," he answers in a serious voice. "Like mine."

Grandpa pokes my stomach. I grab hold of my Grandpa's bent finger. It's true: it's the same thickness and just as hard. Only his finger is rough and scratchy, not smooth like his walking stick.

2.

Grandpa has come to stay. He'll be living with us for a long time. I used to spend all my days with Mama: we looked after the house, and Papa went to work. But recently Mama was asked to go back to her job. She didn't want to at first, but Grandpa insisted. He said he was retired, so it made no difference to him which house he sat around in, but it mattered to Mama that she went back to her job.

"It will be just you and me, all on our own," says Grandpa, leaning over and breathing in my face.

"No, Grandpa," I tell him. "We won't be on our own."

I take Grandpa by the hand and introduce him to my dolls: Katia, who's the daughter, and Nadia, who's the Mama.

Then I introduce him to all my animals: I've got a whole zoo living on the shelf in my closet! And in the gap between the desk and the bed there's a huge stuffed elephant. He was a present from Papa. I show Grandpa how I get on him and hop around the room on his back. Grandpa's noisy leg stomps along next to us.

"See how many of us there are," I say. "There's even your extra leg!"

3.

So, along comes Mama's first day back at work. I catch her dress in the hallway. When Mama is worried about something, her dress flies back and forth around the apartment.

Mama keeps telling Grandpa, "The main thing is to heat up dinner, take her to her painting class . . . and go for walks together. Everything else she manages just fine on her own."

"Of course she does," Grandpa says. "I've never heard of a granddaughter who doesn't get on just fine on her own."

I bounce up and down cheerfully, so Mama sees I'm OK.

"Should I have said no?" Mama asks me. "Maybe I should have stayed home with you a bit longer. It makes no difference for me, but it's a lot for Grandpa. And you'll have to get used to a new routine. . . ."

Grandpa's noisy leg starts tapping impatiently on the parquet floor.

I give Mama a big hug and whisper in her ear. "Everything will be fine! Grandpa and I have a lot in common. He has his third leg, and I have my third hand."

Mama laughs nervously. "Ha ha. And I could do with a third eye. I'd leave it at home to keep an eye on you both. Then I wouldn't worry!"

4.

It's true about my third hand. It's easy at home in our apartment: I can walk around by myself because I know where everything is. I know where the walls are, where the furniture is, which way the doors and cupboards open. But outside it's harder to get around. There aren't walls, and I don't know where everything is. That's why I need someone else's hand when I go for a walk.

I hitch myself onto Grandpa, like a toy wagon hitching onto its locomotive. And Grandpa takes me to my painting class.

"Shoo, shoo. Tok! Shoo, shoo. Tok!"

Grandpa walks along with me, and tells me when to step over a pothole or step around a puddle, and he tells me when the sidewalk ends so I don't trip. I walk along happily. Mama has nothing to worry about. With Grandpa, it's just like normal. Except that Grandpa's third leg sometimes kicks a heap of chestnuts. Or makes other noises I don't recognize.

"What's that?" I ask Grandpa.

It sounds tinkly and crunchy.

"It's the pebbles scattered on the flowerbed," Grandpa explains.

Then there's a muffled, crackly sound.

"And what's that?"

"Some smart aleck didn't take his bag of garbage to the trash can!" Grandpa sounds angry.

Wow-ee! I didn't know that flowerbeds were scattered with pebbles or that people left their trash right outside on the street!

But nothing surprises Grandpa.

"I told you: it's the most useful leg in the world. It tells you everything you need to know."

5.

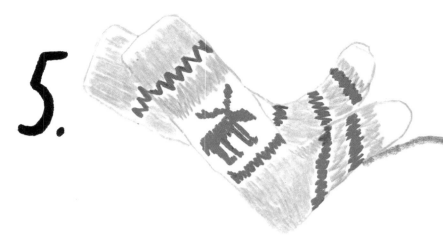

"Grandpa, this is Pasha!" My friend and I come out of our painting class together.

I can't wait to tell him about Grandpa.

"Pasha, my Grandpa has three legs!"

His noisy leg immediately falls to the floor with a crash.

"Oh, I'm sorry," says Pasha.

I realize right away: he must have dropped Grandpa's leg!

"Don't be offended, Grandpa," I ask. "Pasha is always dropping things. Today he dropped his paint again."

"Did it fall on his nose?" Grandpa laughs.

"Again?! Your entire nose is green!" That's Pasha's Mama. "Hello. Come on then, my little prodigy, let's go and wash up. I have to get back to work soon . . ."

Pasha says goodbye and we go outside.

"Shoo, shoo. Tok!"

6.

At home, Grandpa listens to gloomy violin concertos and knits thick, prickly socks to keep his quiet legs and feet warm.

"Grandpa, why don't you knit one for your third leg?" I ask him in between concertos.

"Speedy? She's in too much of a hurry," says Grandpa, his knitting needles knocking together. "Her sock would fall off in no time."

I see what he means. I run my fingers along Speedy and feel how much she wants to run, how she trembles with impatience. Only, she and Grandpa are inseparable: Grandpa never leaves the house without his third leg, and Speedy never leaves the house without Grandpa.

7.

 Tpr-r-r-ru!

"Shoo, shoo. Tok!"

I hold Grandpa's hand. We walk outside, around the block.

"Shoo, shoo. Tok!"

People are running past us, jumping, rollerblading, riding bicycles and even horses. And we're just walking.

"Shoo, shoo. Tok!"

On the second lap around the block, Grandpa says that Speedy's had enough and wants a rest. We stop, and Speedy starts tapping at a puddle. A few happy drops of water jump up at me. It makes me jump, too—I'm so surprised!

"He won't listen to me," complains Grandpa. "Maybe you can get him to calm down?"

He hands me Speedy, but she keeps on splashing in the puddle as hard as she can.

"I can't either," I tell Grandpa, and hand her back.

Grandpa says nothing, and Speedy keeps on splashing around.

Then suddenly I hear: "Tpr-r-r-ru! Tpr-r-r-r-ru!"

The noise is coming from Grandpa! Speedy freezes on the spot— she's so surprised!

"That's how you stop a horse," Grandpa explains. "She just wanted to be a horse."

We carry on walking.

I want to learn how to work out what Speedy's up to!

8.

Being a horse is just the start of it. I soon realize that Speedy can turn into a musician, too.

Sometimes we stop and listen to Speedy's music.

"There are some railings on the left," says Grandpa.

Speedy plays the railings like strings. Her music is different every time, depending on what mood she's in.

One time, it's like rocks falling. . . . Another time, it's like a lonely drum. . . . Sometimes it's not so much like music—it's more like Speedy is muttering something to herself.

That's not all: Speedy can hold the door of the bus open if Grandpa and I don't get on in time. And she knows how to make a breeze stir the pine tree. The trouble is, sometimes pine cones hit me on the head!

But I still like it. When Grandpa and I get tired and have a rest on a bench under the pine tree, there's nothing better than that piney smell in the air.

9.

One day, Grandpa buys me a balloon. There are loads of them to choose from. A huge bunch of them. I look around at all the balloons and choose the one lowest down—because it's closest to me.

But he turns out to be very stubborn! He tries to jump out of my hands.

But I'm paying attention! I hold him tightly on his leash.

We walk along quietly: me with my balloon and Grandpa with Speedy.

Suddenly I hear something wheezy, whizzing in our direction. . . .

It's a dog! Grandpa nudges me behind him. The dog says "Grr-rr-rr!" and grabs Speedy with his teeth! There's a painful crunch. . . . Oh no, poor Speedy!

Someone runs up and pulls the dog away. "How can you not see!" Grandpa says, sounding shocked. "Don't you realize?"

I don't hear what the owner of the dog says; I'm busy looking for Speedy with my hands. There she is! I run my hand over her to calm her down. Where the dog bit her, my fingers feel something rough and spiky. . . .

"Ow!" I shriek and let go of my balloon. He leaps out of my hand.

But at the same second, Speedy jumps up and . . .

"Here," says Grandpa, handing me back my balloon. I'm so happy!

"Hurray, Speedy saved us!" I squeal. "She saved my balloon!! Amazing!"

"I told you that she's the handiest leg in the world!" said Grandpa. "Sweetheart, have you got a splinter? Don't worry, we'll get it out. . . ."

Grandpa and I are laughing so much that we don't even notice that the dog and its owner are gone.

10.

At home, I stick a Band-Aid on our battle wounds: one for Speedy, and one for my finger. Then I ask Grandpa to teach me how to knit.

Even though Speedy doesn't need a sock, I still want to knit her something as a thank you.

"Let me teach you how to make a scarf," Grandpa grinned and showed me how to wrap the wool around my finger, and how to slip the loops onto the other needle.

I had no idea that knitting was so tricky! Grandpa's knitting needles are click-click-clicking away, but mine are wriggling along slowly.

I groan, but I won't give up! After all, Speedy rescued my precious balloon!

I take a long, long time to learn, and finally I knit one long row.

It's OK, Speedy. I promised and I'll do it: your gift is coming!

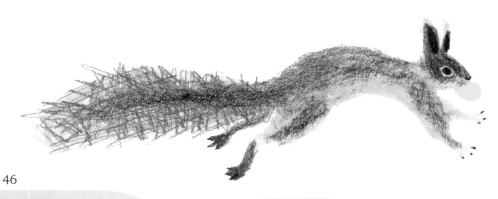

11.

We're walking my Mama to work one day.

"Wow!" she says. "This month has flown by. . . ."

Mama has gotten used to going to work, and I've gotten used to going out with Grandpa.

Speedy has already told us about everything in our neighborhood. So today we decide to go to a park a bit further away.

It rained last night, and the ground is still soft and squidgy under our feet. We walk through the park, and Speedy is quiet for once.

"I'll have to talk for her, today," Grandpa boasts. "Today she's the quietest leg in the world."

Grandpa tells me everything he sees: the shapes of the bushes, how ripe the rosehips are, which way a squirrel ran.

Grandpa explains why the air tastes so good. And sometimes he picks a leaf from a tree, and slips it into my hand.

I guess what each of them is.

This one's chestnut: its leaves are like a hand with its fingers spread out. This one's maple: it's all jagged, like Papa's saw. But I can't tell the difference between the birch leaf and the linden leaf. Grandpa tells me that the birch ones are quite small, and the linden ones are heart-shaped. I'll try to remember that!

We walk for a long time and soon we're right in the middle of the park.

Grandpa remembers that there was a large, old oak tree around here somewhere.

"What kind of leaves does it have?" I ask.

Grandpa looks around, but he can't see any other oak trees around here to show me. He's determined to find that one he remembers.

We wander along different paths until Grandpa stops. He must be tired, I think. But it turns out that he's spotted the oak tree! He stopped to have a quiet look at it.

"Regal as a king," Grandpa says after a moment of silence. "Tall and proud, standing on his own in the clearing, with bushes all around him, like they're his loyal subjects."

Grandpa turns to face the oak tree.

"Your Majesty, we humbly request one leaf. We didn't walk to you for nothing. . . ." Then Grandpa talks to me. "Wait here a minute, my love. The grass is still wet and it's very bumpy. I'll just go and get a leaf. I'll be right back."

I stay on the path, and Grandpa goes to get the leaf. I hear all three of Grandpa's feet say the same thing:

"Squelch, squelch, squelch. . . ."

I hear a loud hoot from Grandpa—he's probably surprised by the new sounds, too.

But no—it turns out that he's slipped and fallen over.

12.

"It hurts to get up," says Grandpa. "I think I've twisted my leg. The quiet one."

I think Grandpa wants to get up, but it sounds like he's trying not to groan.

"What shall we do?" I ask.

"We'll call for help," Grandpa replies. "You start."

"Help!" I call.

"There's no one else around. It's just me and the oak tree here," says Grandpa. "Hmm, what shall we do?"

"Well . . . I'll go," I say, and take two steps to the side. But I stop right away because I don't know how to walk any further.

The trees rustle above me.

"Keep thinking," Grandpa asks.

"I . . . I can walk and wave my arms—then I won't . . . then I won't bump into anything."

"Take Speedy with you," says Grandpa.

I put my hands out and feel Speedy reaching out for them.

"Hold her so she's touching the path, let her walk in front of you, and slowly walk forward," Grandpa explains. "When she's walking on the ground, you'll hear the ground. And if you hear grass on your left, for example, move a bit to the right. And don't worry—I can see where you're going. The paths are quite wide. . . ."

I'm a little afraid, but I do what he says. I gently lower Speedy to the ground, just as my Grandpa said. One step. Two. Three. . . .

"You're doing great—I can see you," comes Grandpa's cheerful voice.

I walk slowly with Speedy, and suddenly I realize that I'm not scared of walking. Speedy and I are holding hands, our fingers are gripping each other. And I think that Grandpa is right: Speedy is the best leg in the world! Because she's not only Grandpa's leg, she can be mine, too! Or anyone's, if they need her.

13.

I turn with the path and I hear footsteps rustling in the distance. I stop and wave.

"Help!"

But no one responds.

"Help!" I repeat loudly.

Someone is running toward me.

"Has something happened to you?" The lady shakes me by the shoulders.

"No," I say.

"Phew. At first I thought you were shouting to someone you knew." The lady is jabbering away. "I was worried about you when I saw you on your own, with a walking stick."

"This is Speedy," I correct the lady. "Grandpa's leg. Grandpa f-fell down and can't get up, and I c-can't help him. . . ."

Suddenly something begins to tremble in my throat.

"Where is he?" asks the lady.

I turn around and point back.

"He's over there," I squeak. "By the oak tree. He slipped and fell over."

"Come on then," says the lady, and she pulls me by the hand.

The woman walks quickly and doesn't warn me about anything, so I keep stumbling. But Speedy runs along as if it's no problem at all.

TOK
tok
toR
ToK
...

14.

Irina—that's the lady's name—calls an ambulance for Grandpa. The doctors say his leg needs rest. They put Grandpa on a stretcher and offer to take us home.

"Thank you so much," says Grandpa as we say goodbye. "What would we have done without you?"

"What would you do without her!" says Irina, putting her arm around my shoulder. "But just don't let her go off on her own again. She is still little. . . ."

"So what?" I say. "I could have gotten anywhere with Speedy."

"Is that right?" Irina sounds surprised.

But I know Speedy agrees!

15.

In the evening, Mama and Papa do a lot of sighing.

"I haven't been around enough," Papa says to Grandpa.

"I shouldn't have gone back to work," says Mama.

"It's all right," Grandpa and I say together, and Speedy agrees.

I show Mama and Papa how I walked along with Speedy in the park—as if I were all on my own! Speedy knocks against the doorframe.

"See? He finds things that are in the way," I explain to my Mama and Papa. "But in the park, the paths were wide, and there was nothing in my way."

Grandpa snorts beside me.

"She needs her own Speedy," he says, sounding proud.

"Not a Speedy," says Papa. "You need your own special walking stick."

16.

In the evening I lie in bed and imagine myself getting my own walking stick, so I can walk on my own. Only not right away. Papa said it'll take a long time to learn. But all the same, I'll be able to walk on my own, without a third hand. I know it's not scary. It's just like with Speedy.

And then Grandpa and I will be even more alike: he'll have three legs and I'll have three legs.

I can't sleep because I'm thinking so much. So, I get up quietly, leave my room, and sneak into the living room. I find the ball of wool and knitting needles, get comfy in my chair, and finish my scarf. Tomorrow I'll give it to Speedy. I know how happy she'll be and exactly what she'll say.

"Tok! Tok! Tok!"

1.

One stick. Another stick. Another stick. Then another stick. It's an M!

That's me writing on the chalkboard. I write on my board every day. Mama painted it with black paint. And I write on it with chalk. Any word I want.

Now the letter U. Mama is making breakfast. I don't know what we're having today.

She and I have a game we play: she comes up with breakfast and I come up with a word. And then we both work out what it is.

Now the letter S. Actually, I also have ready-made letters. They're small magnets that stick to the fridge. They're clean and don't make your hands mucky like chalk. But Mama says that making words with magnet letters isn't the same as writing them by myself.

Now I. Poor little thing. Just one stick. No one spends much time with I, because he's so quick to write. So I'm going to give him an extra BIG dot.

Now C. Oh no, I've done it again. I've forgotten where I started!

I mustn't do a whole circle. C is just half a circle. Hmm, I think I'll stop there.

There we are: C.

"Done!" I call to Mama.

"M-u-s-i-c," reads Mama.

"You got it!" I shout.

And I take a sniff.

"Are we having porridge today?

"Yes!" Mama answers.

So I guessed right, too!

Then we sing our song:

♪ Porridge, porridge, porridge ♪

♪ Yummy, yummy porridge ♪

We sing like the birds outside. Because the birds in our garden love oats like us—especially the sparrows! Even though they have theirs cold, not cooked with milk like we do.

The sparrows in the garden sing ♪ chirp-chirp-cheep ♪

And the yellowhammers sing ♪ twee-twoo-tweet ♪

It's nice of them to join in our porridge song, even though they don't know the words that Mama and I sing.

♪ Porridge, porridge, porridge ♪

♪ Yummy, yummy porridge ♪

2.

Twee-
tWee-
TWeet!

Today, Mama and I are going to a concert. After breakfast, we take a bus downtown. I ask Mama where we're getting off.

"We'll get off at the Theater bus stop," says Mama. "The one after Pushkin Street."

We ride the bus and I listen to the announcements. I don't like buses that don't tell you the names of the stops. It's rude. I get offended when the bus doesn't talk to me. Then I chat with Mama or Papa the whole way, so the bus hears me and joins in.

But this bus is one of the polite ones. When we hear it say "Theater," Mama and I jump off the bus and walk to the theater. It's a long walk! So when we get there, we don't feel like going up the stairs, and we wait for the elevator.

It turns out that the elevator is also nice and polite.

"First floor," says the elevator, and the doors open.

We go in.

"Which floor are we going to?" I ask Mama and I reach forward.

"Um, the third floor," Mama says, thinking. She takes my hand and leads it to the buttons. "Look, here are the numbers, the numerals 1, 2, 3 . . ."

I touch them.

"Yeah! Like my magnets."

I know the numbers! I've got number magnets like this at home that go with my letter magnets.

"And underneath the numbers are dots—see?" asks Mama. "They're also numbers. They're just written differently."

I touch them, but I don't understand. Mama must have gotten muddled up.

"No, Mama, they're not numbers," I tell her. "They're some kind of bumpy bubbles."

I press the 3 button, and up we go.

3.

Mama and I lie back on our cushions and listen to the harp. Today's concert is in a little room. It's so small that I can follow the wall all the way around. Not like the Philharmonic, where Grandpa and I go. The halls there are enormous, and there's rustling and creaking and muttering all around you. And the music just flies up somewhere under the ceiling.

Here, there's only the sound of one harp, vibrating all around, even in the cushions. I listen to the harp with one ear and the cushion with the other. And it's as if the harp's song is inside me. It climbs into my belly and tickles me. It's beautiful. Like our porridge song.

After the concert, my mother and I go over to touch the harp. It's lopsided and full of long strings. Mama says the harp looks like a huge bird with slender feathers.

"I wonder if there's really a bird this shape?"

"Why don't we go to the library and have a look?" Mama suggests. "It's not far from here."

"Huh? Do they keep birds there?" I'm amazed.

"No, but they have special books with lots of birds in them," says Mama. "You're not too tired?"

"No!" I say and I flap my arms about. "Look, my wings are full of energy!"

4.

I love reading books. I have two whole shelves in my room and one of them is full of books. They all feel similar, with smooth, thin pages. They're the ones Mama reads to me at night.

And during the day I listen to books on CD. They live on the second shelf. They're all in square boxes that feel the same, but each one has a different sticker.

Grandpa and I put a house sticker on *Karlsson on the Roof*. We stuck a flower on *The Scarlet Flower*, and an elephant on *38 Parrots* because it's got Little Elephant in it. Grandpa and I labeled each CD with a sticker, and now I never get them muddled up.

I take whichever one I want, put the CD in the player, press the "play" button and listen.

I wonder what kind of bird books they have in the library. Paper ones or CD ones?

Mama asks me to sit in an armchair while she goes off for a minute. Then she comes back with someone.

"Well, who's this that has come to see us?" asks a lady who I don't know. She's smiling at me. I can hear it.

"It's me," I say. "And Mama."

"And my name's Natalya," she says with an even bigger smile.

"I'm here to read books with everyone who visits," Natalya explains. "Have you read anything by a writer called Vitaly Bianki?"

"No," I say.

"Great!" says Natalya. "Let's go inside our little reading house."

Mama and I follow Natalya, and we really do come to a little house. Wow! A whole little house inside the library. A building inside a building! I walk around it: the little house has three windows and one door.

"Come in, and have a seat," says Natalya.

We go inside, and we're in a small room.

There's a sofa and a table with a CD player. Natalya presses play and we all listen to the story together. Bianki's birds are so argumentative! They spend the whole time bickering about which of them has the best nose!

"Great! Now let's have a look at the pictures," says Natalya.

She places a box in front of me.

"Open it up."

I take out a board covered with pieces of different kinds of fabric. Like a canvas from art class.

"What's this?"

"It's the two sandpiper brothers, remember?"

Natalya takes my fingers and runs them along the birds. One is taller, and the other is smaller. I can feel their legs and heads. And there are their feathers and their long thin noses. One nose is pointing up, and the other one is going down.

"Just like in the book!"

"That's right. It's a picture of the book. Now, let's see the other one. So. . . . Who's this?"

Wow, what a big bird! It has rubbery legs. It has a long neck and a bag around its neck. Oh, it's got a pocket! And there's something in it!

"It's the pelican with his fish in the bag!" I shout. "He's got his packed lunch with him for later!"

"That's right," confirms Natalya.

And the fish is tiny, but he's a fast swimmer. He zips straight into my hand to hide.

"Now the pelican can't eat it!"

"And who's sitting in the tree?" asks Natalya.

I have a look: just a nose, just a head, just a tail, just feathers.

"I don't know . . ."

"What a funny way to sit," says Mama.

And it really is funny. Its feet are against the tree, and so is its beak.

"Ah, I know! It's the woodpecker hammering away at the tree!"

"That's right!" says Natalya, her voice full of praise.

We sit there for such a long time looking at all the birds. It's a pity they don't have a bird as huge as the harp in this book. But maybe the harp bird isn't argumentative enough to be in this story.

"So, what did you do at the library?" ask Papa and Grandpa when we get home.

"I was looking at the birds," I said. "They were arguing about who has the best nose."

I pull the bowl of seeds toward me. Then I cross my first finger over my thumb to make a beak, and poke about in the cup.

"Guess what I am!"

"A bullfinch?" asks Papa.

"A spotted nutcracker?" asks Grandpa.

"No! It's a crossbill! See? His beak crosses over. He can get all the seeds out of a pine cone. Now who am I . . . ?"

I pick up my bag and hang it round my neck.

"What do you think? I've got a bag under my beak. I hide fish in it—plop!"

And I shove a spoon in the bag.

"A pelican?" Papa is the first to guess.

"You got it!" I shout. "OK, who am I now?"

I go over to the door, hold onto it, and poke my nose at it.

"That looks just like a woodpecker!" says Grandpa.

"You got it!" I yell again.

And then I bang my nose against the door!
"Ow!"

Papa comes over to give me a hug. He kisses me on the nose.

"And if I were a bird, I wouldn't argue with you. I know for a fact that your nose is the best!

6.

Now we often go to Natalya's library. I love the special books they have there. They're called tactile books. Probably because they're made up of lots of pieces of fabric like tiles in a mosaic.

This one has tiles in a triangle shape . . . that's how a flock of birds flies across the sky. These tiles are thin lines going down and across . . . that's the rain. There's so much inside these tactile books.

But my favorite one is the book *The Snow Queen*. It has a little Gerda doll in it. You can take her wandering through the pages looking for Kai.

First, Gerda meets the wise Raven, who is hiding in the bushes. Then there's the robber, who jumps out with his pistol if you open the page quickly!

And then there's the reindeer. He has lovely, soft fur. I could stroke it forever and ever.

I piece together the jigsaw puzzle of the house, and then Kai is freed from the spell! I turn the page—and now there are two dolls! Gerda and Kai.

Then one day Natalya says:

"You see how different books can be. You can listen with your ears, or you can look at the pictures with your hands. But you know . . . you can also read a book with your fingers."

And she hands me a book made of thick sheets full of dots.

I've seen these dots before somewhere. . . . Oh, I remember!

"It's the bumpy bubbles from the elevator!"

"That's right! These bumpy bubbles are a special way of writing so you can read with your fingers," says Natalya, with a smile in her voice. "All the letters are written with dots."

I slide my fingers over the dots. How are you supposed to read it? I can't understand a thing!

"You'll get to know each letter one by one," Natalya explains. "Here, I'll give you a slate and stylus. This is for you to write the letters and start to recognize them. With time, you'll learn to read."

But I push the book away, and pick up Kai and Gerda again.

"Gerda, can it be my turn to save you now?" Kai suggests.

That's more fun! I don't want to read those silly bumpy bubbles. What's the point of them?

7.

The slate is two layers attached with a hinge. One layer has tiny windows, and the other one has little holes, or dips, like craters. And the stylus is like a stick with a beak. Papa puts some paper between the two layers and with the stylus he pecks at the little holes through the windows.

"That's right!" says Natalya. "Wonderful!"

Natalya gives us a plastic sheet with the alphabet in dots. And Papa's learning to write them on paper.

"Let's see. What have we got?"

Papa takes the paper sheet out from between the two layers and turns it over. I have a look with my fingers.

"It's not anything!"

It's just bumps. Nothing but bumps! Not like my magnet letters. Not like the letters I write on the blackboard. Those letters are all different! And these dots are all the same.

But Papa says, "It works! Look, this is A."

"A is three sticks," I disagree.

"A is also one dot," says Papa, refusing to give up. "Go on, have a go at writing it. It'll help you learn it. Then that's one done—25 to go!"

I reluctantly pick up the stylus, and Papa shows me.

"In each window, there are six holes. Two at the top, two in the middle, and two at the bottom. The hole for A is the top right.

I poke the stylus into the holes.

"A, A, A, A."

"Listen—your stylus is like a woodpecker!" Papa laughs.

It's true. It's a woodpecker hammering his beak on the slate.

A A A A

"Poor woodpecker," I say to Papa. "He must be getting bored, just tapping the same place over and over."

I do a few more As. And then I have an idea.

"Papa, let's give the woodpecker another letter."

"Good idea," Papa agrees. "Let's give him a B. That's two dots. It's got one where the letter A is. And the other one in the hole beneath the A.

I'm hammering the stylus through the windows:

"B, B, B, B."

A B B A

B A A A

Don't worry, woodpecker. I won't let you get bored!

8.

First, Papa and I learned the letter with one dot: A

Then we learned all the letters with two dots:

B C E I K

Then we learned all the letters with three dots:

D F H J L M O S U

Then all the letters with four dots:

G N P R T V W X Z

Then the letters with five dots: Q Y

And there aren't any with six dots!

That's it!

After practicing for a while, my fingers remember how to read all of the letters of the alphabet!

And now I can write my own words: Mama, Papa, Grandpa, music, book, woodpecker. . . . What a lot of amazing words!

I take the sheet of paper out from the slate, so I can read my "Mama, Papa, Grandpa, music, book, woodpecker . . ." but somehow I can't understand anything. It's just a jumble of dots and I can't separate one letter from another at all!

The dots aren't doing what they're supposed to! They're getting all muddled up under my fingers.

They're still just silly little bumps, and I can't understand a thing! It's so annoying!

"You're just like Speedy," says Grandpa, clicking his knitting needles. "Always in a rush! But reading takes time, and lots of practice. Why don't you start with some short words? Try a little one, like "yes" for example. Write that first, then read it—just one word at a time. That's how you'll learn, little by little."

But I'm so annoyed, I don't want to read anything! I put another sheet of paper in the slate, and I poke the stylus through all the holes in the windows!

The paper turns out all bumpy like a rug. I run my fingers over it. It's beautiful and easy to understand. Without any silly words.

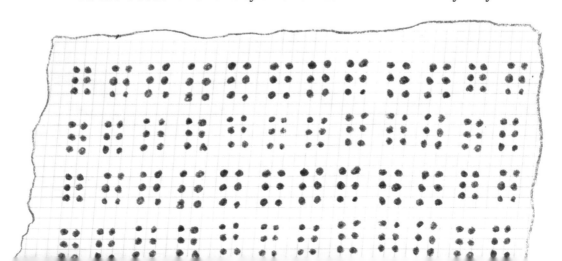

9.

"Pasha, would you like to learn a secret code?" asks Papa.

What? What's he talking about?

"Actually, Pasha is here to see me!" I tell Papa.

But Pasha is curious. Of course he wants to know what Papa's talking about.

"A secret code?" He throws his jacket on the floor, too excited to hang it up. "Yes, please!"

"Let's do secret codes for a bit," he says to me. "And then go and play?"

"I'm sure your host will agree," says Mama, stroking my head.

"OK," I mutter.

Papa shows Pasha the alphabet sheet, the slate, and the stylus.

"Look at this. This is the code. And this is where you can write different words."

Papa taps out something, then takes the sheet of paper and gives it to Pasha.

"Can you work it out?"

Pasha breathes heavily as he works it out.

"H . . . E . . . L . . . L . . . O . . . P . . . A . . . S . . . H . . . HELLO PASHA!"

"Let me check," I say, and I take the sheet.

He's right: Pasha! There's a P and next to it there's an A. Then an S, an H, and another A.

Well, look at that! I was confused by the letters for ages, and he just read it right away!"

"But you know all the letters," says Papa. "So you can teach Pasha yourself."

"Come on, teach me the code!" says Pasha, impatient.

"It's not a code!" I say.

"What do you mean?" Pasha is surprised.

Then I take my stylus and I write . . .

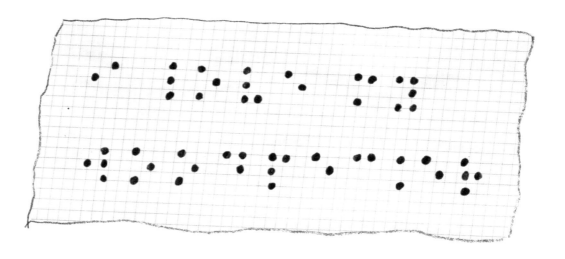

10.

♪ Peck, peck, peck, peck, peck, peck, peck . . . ♪

　♪ My woodpecker loves to peck . . . ♪

Now when I write notes to Pasha, I sing along.

　♪ Peck, peck, peck, peck, peck, peck, peck . . . ♪

And Pasha has his own slate and stylus now. We pass notes to each other in art class. No one else can understand what they say. Because no one else knows how to write like we do!

　♪ Peck, peck, peck, peck, peck, peck, peck . . . ♪

I've already written half a page! It takes ages, of course. But it's beautiful, like a song.

　♪ Peck, peck, peck, peck, peck, peck, peck . . . ♪

And if Pasha gets his letters muddled up, it's OK—I can help him work it out.

1.

For New Year's, Mama and Papa gave me a huge rubber ring! It's like a gigantic doughnut! The ring kind, not the kind with jam in the middle. In the middle is where you sit!

"Come on, let's inflate it!"

My inflatable doughnut is in the box. It's thin and floppy. Like a deflated balloon.

Papa takes the pump and pumps it up with air. And soon the bouncy ring fills every inch of floor space in the room!

"It's enormous!" I exclaim.

I climb into the middle of my doughnut, and lie back against the side.

"Mama, look! I'm out at sea."

"Do you remember how we swam in the sea last summer?" asks Mama.

"Of course I do!"

Mama and Papa swam on their own. And I had a dolphin.

The dolphin was my buoyancy aid. It had squidgy eyes and puffy fins. I had so much fun swimming with him! Two fins and two hands. And we swam all the way to the end of the swimming area! There were funny balls bobbing about on a rope. Guarding the sea. Papa said they're called buoys. Not like the boys I know.

They weren't at all boisterous! No, they just bobbed quietly on the spot—buk, buk, buk—and that's it.

The dolphin and I swayed with the buoys for a while. To keep them company.

And then Papa pulled us along behind him like a tugboat.

Now in our apartment, Papa's pulling my doughnut along by the rope. I lie there, my feet bouncing up and down on the side. Poom! Poom! Poom!

It's so springy! It's like my dolphin has grown bigger and fatter and stronger. . . .

"Mama, Papa, I know!" I shout. "It's not a giant doughnut. . . .

It's a whale!"

2.

My whale has been living on the balcony for two weeks now. So our balcony is like a fish tank. But whales live in the huge, deep oceans, not tiny tanks.

We've only got a balcony. It's not enough room for a huge whale: he needs space to swim around. The poor thing.

I open the door and my whale waves to me with his fin. Every whale has a triangular fin on its back—that's its dorsal fin.

My Grandpa and I have read lots about whales. And we've looked at the pictures in the library. And we've listened to recordings of whales singing to each other.

"Oo! Eee-oo! Vee-oo!" That's how they talk. By singing. That's how my whale and I talk to each other.

"Papa, when can we take my whale out for a ride?"

"Soon," Papa answers. "This weekend."

I shake the whale's fin and translate Papa's words for him:

"Mee-oo! Aoo!"

Then we both sigh together: "Eee-oo! Eee-oo!"

The weekend is days away! Such a long time to wait! Maybe that's how deep the ocean is: as deep as a long, long wait.

3.

Hurray, it's finally the weekend! Papa and I are taking my whale out for a ride in the snow today!

We're going to the forest park, to slide down the banks onto the frozen creek. Papa pulls us along by the rope. My whale slides along in the snow. I hold on to his fin with one hand, and with the other hand I reach out and touch the snow with my mitten.

The snow is as soft as fluff and as hard as a rock. But my whale doesn't mind. He swims along happily, delighted to be out of his tank. And Papa whistles along happily. As if he caught my whale with his fishing rod!

"All right, here's the creek," he says. "Let's drop the anchor." And he drops his backpack onto the snow.

We're here! I clap my mittens. I love this creek. Although he's a bit of a scaredy cat. He's just a little stream really, and he's always hiding away behind his high banks.

But in winter, the creek banks turn into slides. And everyone comes to ride on their sleds and rubber rings. And I'm going to ride my whale!

"Hold on to the handles," says Papa.

"The fins," I remind him.

"Hold on to the fins," Papa says. "First I'll make sure there's no one in the way, then I'll push you off."

My whale and I are waiting. We're very patient. We've been waiting for two whole weeks! But soon we hear Papa shout:

"Ready? Ready to dive down to the bottomless ocean?"

"Ooh! Ooh!" we sing—my whale and I.

Papa lets go, and we whoosh down the slide! Whoo!

The wind takes my voice away. And my heart dives into my belly. It's hiding in my belly like the stream hides in its banks.

But I don't have time to be scared—it's all so fast! Before we know it, my whale is at the bottom of the sea! Hello, snowy ocean!

4.

I'm diving deep into the ocean on my whale and helping him find some friends.

"Who have you found this time?" Papa shouts from above the surface.

"An octopus!" I yell, and I wave my arms and legs. "Here are my first four legs!"

Then I wave my arms and legs again. "And here are my other four legs! I've got eight legs!"

"What a wonderful friend!" Papa approves.

Then I take my whale by the rope and turn to Papa and climb up the bank. Papa encourages me.

"That's it, Octopus, you can do it. One more step. . . . Great, up you come!"

And off we go again . . . wheeeee!

"What's new down there in the ocean?" Papa yells from up on the shore.

I lie back on my whale and introduce our new friend.

"We've met a nice crab!"

Our whale is lucky! He's already met an orange turtle, a pikey fish, a seahorse, an octopus, and now a nice crab!

"We'll be opening an aquarium at this rate," says Papa. "An oceanarium!"

I drag my whale up the bank again.

Then off we go again. . . . Wheeeee. . . . Splash!

We're back at the bottom of the ocean. But suddenly, instead of Papa's voice, I hear someone else calling me from up close.

"And now the whale has found a beautiful mermaid!" she says. "Shall we slide down together?"

I climb off of my whale.

"Can I touch you?" I ask her.

"Yes," says the mermaid.

I see what she looks like: woolly hat with a pompom, long hair. . . . Wow, she really is a beautiful mermaid! I'll call her Rusalka!

"Yeah!" I shout. "Let's slide down together!"

And I tell Papa:

"And now my whale has found Rusalka—a lovely mermaid!"

"Wonderful!" answers Papa. "Come on up together!"

And the three of us climb up the bank.

Rusalka flops onto my whale with me, and I feel a bit squashed.

"Can the whale hold us both?" I ask Papa.

"Oh yes, he's strong enough for the two of you," says Papa. "Grab the fins."

I grab the fin on one side, but I can't reach the other side, because Rusalka's there.

"Ready? Steady? . . ."

Go! . . .

Wheeeee . . .

Splash!

We dive into the ocean. I'm wobbling from side to side because it's hard to hold on to just one fin. But Rusalka is squealing so much, my heart is pounding with joy. Bo-bum! Bo-bum!

I also start squealing along with her. But then we fall out on the snow!

"Let's do it again!" Rusalka says, laughing.

"Yeah, let's go!" I say, and brush the snow off my face with my mitten.

Rusalka runs ahead, and I can't keep up with her.

Then she comes back, takes my hand, and pulls me up the slope. Me and the whale! That's how strong she is!

Before I even catch my breath, we sit down again and grab the fins. And hold hands.

We slide down again, huddled up together—it's much cozier that way and we don't wobble around so much!

And we squeal in our two voices: "Eee-yee-yee! Eee-yee-yee!"

I'm sure that's how mermaids communicate. Like whales with their songs and calls.

And we both know what that means. It means:

"Hurray!"

"Hurray!"

6.

Rusalka and I are lying at the bottom of the ocean, laughing.

Suddenly, someone nearby calls:

"Veronica! Come here!"

Rusalka jumps off our whale, and drags us to the side.

"Grandma, I'm a mermaid riding on a whale!" cries Rusalka. Ah, so she's actually called Veronica.

But her grandma isn't happy.

"Listen to me," says her grandma. "Come here!"

The mermaid stops, hands me the rope, and goes over to her grandma.

"What are you playing at?" I hear her grandma getting angry. "Can't you see how the little girl is? And there you are dragging her back and forth like that. What if something were to happen?! You're older than her and you don't understand. She's got enough on her plate!"

Rusalka the mermaid huffs. Then, in a fancy, cheerful voice, her grandma calls over to me.

"You dear little thing!"

And then she speaks angrily to Rusalka again.

"Time to go home. You're already as wet as a drowned rat."

"I'm not a rat!" says Rusalka, whimpering. "I don't want to go home!"

"Let's go and slide on the other side," says her grandma. "At least there's a bench there. I want to put my feet up!"

"OK!" says Rusalka, sounding happy again.

"That's good," says her grandma, who sounds cheerful now. Then she puts on that fancy voice again. "Say goodbye to the little girl."

"Goodbye!" says Rusalka, and she runs up and gives me such a big hug that we both fall over in the snow.

"What did I just tell you about getting wet?!" her grandma exclaims.

Then Rusalka the mermaid goes. And I'm here on my own.

"Whale!" Papa shouts from the top of the slide. "Did you get caught in a net? Or have you caught another friend?"

7.

Without Rusalka, I'm really slow to climb up the bank again. My giant rubber ring feels like an elephant!

"Oh," Papa wonders. "Is the whale tired?"

"No," I say.

"And the whale's hands and feet aren't frozen?" asks Papa.

"No," I answer.

"Shall we stop and have some nice warm tea?" asks Papa.

And I ask, "Why did Rusalka's grandma say such a strange thing?"

"What did she say?" asks Papa.

"She said I've 'got enough on my plate.' What did she mean?"

Then Papa snorts.

"Pfft! What's so strange about saying that? Of course you've got enough on your plate!"

Papa pours the tea from the thermos, and takes a noisy sip.

"You have plenty of good things in your life. Look at me—that's one! Then there's clever Mama who's made us yummy tea with buns—that's two! Then there's Grandpa, with Speedy—that makes three! And your whale. . . ."

That does sound like enough. Too much, even! But sorry, whale, I'm the only one who gets tea and buns on my plate.

"Well, Papa, you've got enough on your plate, too," I argue. "You've got Mama! And Grandpa! We all have enough. We all have lots! So we should share everything and make it fair."

"All right, you got it," Papa agrees, and hands me a mug.

Yay! Tea with currant jam! My favorite!

I'm so excited that I jump up, and splash some tea on my whale.

Ee-oo! Voo-oo!

But he's not complaining. He's lying in the snow and feeling happy that he's got some on his plate, too. Have a little rest, whale. We'll go out looking for friends again soon.

8.

We're home now. And it smells like perfume! I know who's come to visit: it's Taika!

"So, how was it?" Mama asks. "Did you get soaked?"

"We met a mermaid! Rusalka! We went diving on my whale together! But then her grandma took her away because I had enough on my plate."

Taika sighs loudly.

"Tell me about it . . ." says Papa, and sighs along with Taika. "She was a nice little girl who came running along to play with her. They were sliding down the bank happily, and then. . . ."

Papa sounds angry for some reason. But I don't have time to think about it. I want to show Taika my whale.

"Look—isn't he great?"

"Well, well, well . . ." says Taika. "Some people think whales swim alone—the ocean is so huge, after all. . . . But no! Whales can hear each other from hundreds of miles away . . . and they understand each other."

"And Rusalka understood my whale today!" I say. "Right, Papa?"

"They're the ones who'll save the world!" Taika laughs. "The mermaids!"

But Mama protests.

"No mermaids, please! As if people weren't enough . . ."

And then Mama says to me. "Come on, my deep-sea diver, let's put your rubber ring on the balcony."

And I roll my whale into his tank, and sing to her in our language.

"Voo-oo! Wasn't that fun today?"

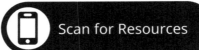

Scan for Resources

Acknowledgments

The first story, *The Invisible Elephant*, was published as a picture book in 2013. Thank you to everyone who met the elephant then and made friends with him. Many readers were excited to see him grow up. And here he is—he's grown up into an entire chapter book! I would especially like to thank Yulia and Svetlana Vasiliev, Viktoria Yashkova, and Yekaterina Chupachina for their invaluable expertise and advice; the staff at the children's department of St. Petersburg Library for the Blind and Visually Impaired for introducing me to tactile books; Anna Godiner, researcher into books about children with disabilities, for her support; and my editor Anna Stern for her strong desire to publish this book. Thank you! Your support helped me in writing these stories. My particular thanks go to my editor Natalia Kaloshina, to the artist Yulia Sidneva, and the entire team at Samokat publishing house—for creating the Russian edition of this book.

ABOUT THE AUTHOR

ANNA ANISIMOVA is the author of over 10 books and has been shortlisted for several literary prizes. A picture book version of "The Invisible Elephant"—one of the four stories in this collection—was selected by The International Board on Books for Young People (IBBY) for their 2017 list "Outstanding Books for Young People with Disabilities."

ABOUT THE ILLUSTRATOR

YULIA SIDNEVA is an artist and illustrator, and a member of the Moscow Union of Artists. She graduated from the Moscow State University of Printing. In addition to illustrating children's books Sidneva also designs various printed products, gives master classes in book graphics, and works as a designer at Samokat Publishing House.

ABOUT THE TRANSLATOR

RUTH AHMEDZAI KEMP is a literary translator working from Arabic, German and Russian into English. She translates fiction and non-fiction, and has a particular interest in history, historical fiction, and writing for children and young adults. Her translations include books from Germany, Jordan, Morocco, Palestine, Russia, Switzerland and Syria. Her translation of *The Raven's Children* by Yulia Yakovleva was recognized in the 2022 IBBY Honor List.

ABOUT YONDER

YONDER is an imprint from Restless Books devoted to bringing the wealth of great stories from around the globe to English-reading children, middle-graders, and young adults. Books from other countries, cultures, viewpoints, and storytelling traditions can open up a universe of possibility, and the wider our view, the more powerfully books enrich and expand us. In an increasingly complex, globalized world, stories are potent vehicles of empathy. We believe it is essential to teach our kids to place themselves in the shoes of others beyond their communities, and instill in them a lifelong curiosity about the world and their place in it. Through publishing a diverse array of transporting stories, Yonder nurtures the next generation of savvy global citizens and lifelong readers.